LORI DITTMER

COWS

CREATIVE EDUCATION · CREATIVE PAPERBACKS

Published by Creative Education
and Creative Paperbacks
P.O. Box 227, Mankato, Minnesota 56002
Creative Education and Creative Paperbacks are
imprints of The Creative Company
www.thecreativecompany.us

Design by Ellen Huber
Production by Colin O'Dea
Art direction by Rita Marshall
Printed in the United States of America

Photographs by Alamy (Hemis, imageBROKER),
iStockphoto (ablokhin, alberto clemares expósito,
curtoicurto, DaveLongMedia, debibishop, emholk,
Global_Pics, GlobalP, GoodLifeStudio, Jevtic, JMichl,
ktmoffitt, Diane Kuhl, Lakeview_Images, malerapaso,
pixdeluxe, Pixelsatwork, shaunl, Pavel Sipachev,
Stulloyd100, ToprakBeyBetmen, Phichit Wongsunthi,
xjben), Shutterstock (Anton Havelaar, Svietlieisha
Olena, Zeljko Radojko)

Copyright © 2020 Creative Education, Creative Paperbacks
International copyright reserved in all countries.
No part of this book may be reproduced in any form
without written permission from the publisher.

Library of Congress Cataloging-in-Publication Data
Names: Dittmer, Lori, author.
Title: Cows / Lori Dittmer.
Series: Grow with me.
Includes bibliographical references and index.
Summary: An explanation of the life cycle and life span
of cows, using up-close photographs and step-by-step
text to follow a cow's growth process from embryo to
calf to mature cow.

Identifiers: ISBN 978-1-64026-230-0 (hardcover)
ISBN 978-1-62832-793-9 (pbk)
ISBN 978-1-64000-365-1 (eBook)
This title has been submitted for CIP processing under
LCCN 2019938370.

CCSS: RI.3.1, 2, 3, 4, 5, 6, 7, 8; RI.4.1, 2, 3, 4, 5, 7; RF.3.3, 4

First Edition HC 9 8 7 6 5 4 3 2 1
First Edition PBK 9 8 7 6 5 4 3 2 1

TABLE OF CONTENTS

Cattle	4
Horns and Hooves	7
Bovine Babies	8
Springtime Calving	11
Growing Up	12
Cud-Chewers	14
Stomach Chambers	17
Cattle Reproduction	18
Safety in Numbers	21
Staying Healthy	22
Auroch Ancestors	25
Cows and Humans	26
Death of a Cow	28
Life Cycle	30
Glossary	31
Websites	32
Read More	32
Index	32

CATTLE

Cattle are **mammals** called ruminants. Ruminants have hooves and special stomachs. Cattle have four stomach chambers to help them **digest** food. Females are called cows. Males are bulls. But many people refer to all cattle as cows.

Cattle live on farms all around the world. Many of the world's cattle live in India and Brazil. They eat grass and feed made from grains. Farmers take care of these animals.

Spanish fighting bulls are known for their aggressive behavior.

The horns of a Texas longhorn can measure eight feet (2.4 m) in length.

HORNS AND HOOVES

Cows are different colors, depending on their **breed**. They can be white, black, red, or brown. Some have horns. The horns of a Texas longhorn stick out to each side. Spanish fighting bulls' horns curve forward. Angus are **polled** cattle.

Cow hooves are divided into two toes. This helps them support their heavy bodies. A cow can weigh 1,600 pounds (726kg) or more!

Each half of a cow's hoof is also known as a claw.

BOVINE BABIES

A baby cow starts out as a tiny **embryo** (*EM-bree-oh*). As it grows, it becomes known as a fetus. The mother cow is pregnant for about nine months. The fetus gains about 80 pounds (36.3 kg) during the last 3 months.

Farmers feed pregnant cows extra food. This helps the baby grow. Often, farmers keep expectant mothers in special pens. These are clean and safe places for the cows to give birth.

Dairy cows eat about 100 pounds (45.4 kg) of food each day.

A pregnant cow carries a male calf for a slightly longer period than a female calf.

(10) *Mother cows lick their newborn calves to clean and dry them.*

SPRINGTIME CALVING

A mother cow gives birth to one baby, called a calf. Sometimes cows have twins. Calves are usually born in the spring. A cow and her calf moo to each other. Each knows the sound of the other's voice.

Most cows give birth every 12 to 14 months. A female calf is called a heifer. A male is a bull calf.

GROWING UP

At birth, a calf weighs about 90 pounds (40.8 kg). It drinks its mother's milk right away. A calf stands up and walks within an hour of birth. Calves are born with milk teeth. After about one week, calves might nibble grass and grains. They drink lots of water, too.

Calves gain about two pounds (907 g) per day. They love to run and play together in the **pasture**. Farmers usually **wean** calves between the ages of two and eight months.

Young calves need to spend about a quarter of the day resting.

It takes several weeks before a calf's stomach is fully ready to handle solid food.

CUD-CHEWERS

Cows chew their cud about 40 to 50 times in a minute.

Adult cows eat more than 25 pounds (11.3 kg) of food each day. By age 2, cows have 32 teeth. But they have no teeth in the upper front gum. Like all ruminants, cows have a firm dental pad. This helps them pull grass from the ground.

A cow chews just a few times to moisten its food. Then it swallows. Later, the cow **regurgitates** partially digested food known as cud. The cow chews its cud in a side-to-side motion.

Large eyes and oval pupils let cows see in almost all directions.

15

16 — Cows feel less stress and move together when kept in a herd.

STOMACH CHAMBERS

Cows spend most of the day eating and chewing cud. When a cow swallows, food travels to the rumen. This is the largest pouch in the stomach. In the rumen, food mixes with fluid to form cud. When a cow swallows its cud, the food travels through the four parts of its stomach.

The cow's stomach absorbs the **nutrients** from its food. Cows eat grass, as well as the leaves and stems of other plants. These are hard for other animals to digest.

Farmers often grow nutritious alfalfa to feed their cattle.

CATTLE REPRODUCTION

Some farms raise only female cattle. Others might keep a bull. When a heifer is about two years old, she is ready to have her own calf.

Bulls can be aggressive. They might fight each other. Often, farmers use **artificial** methods to make their cows pregnant. Then they do not need to keep a bull.

A metal nose ring allows farmers to handle a bull more easily.

19

20　Cows in a herd tend to face the same direction as they eat.

SAFETY IN NUMBERS

Cows gather in herds for safety. A cow shows its mood with its tail. If the tail hangs straight down, it means the cow is relaxed. If a cow tucks its tail between its legs, it might be sick or scared.

Cows have a good sense of smell. They can detect scents up to six miles (9.7 km) away! Cows' eyes are on the sides of their heads. This helps them see threats coming from behind. Cows also have good memories. They recognize the people who take care of them.

Cattle need space to find food and shelter to protect them from bad weather.

STAYING HEALTHY

Cows can develop skin **infections**. They can suffer from lung diseases, too. Bloat is a common illness. When a cow eats certain grasses too quickly, gas builds up in its stomach.

Farmers must check their herds regularly. They make sure that their animals stay healthy.

Ringworm is a common infection that makes skin itchy and sore.

Cattle remember and are more responsive to people who treat them well.

23

24 *France's Lascaux caves feature roughly 600 prehistoric paintings.*

AUROCH ANCESTORS

Heck cattle were bred in an attempt to bring back aurochs.

Today's cattle likely came from aurochs. These wild cattle were larger than modern cattle. Ancient cave drawings in France and Italy show animals that could be aurochs. These animals died out a long time ago.

People have raised cattle for thousands of years. When people settled in new lands, they brought cows with them. Throughout the 1800s, most families owned a cow.

COWS AND HUMANS

People raise cows for many reasons. Cow milk is used in dairy products. Some people eat beef. Cowhide is made into leather. It is then used for furniture, clothing, and sports equipment. Soap, lipstick, and crayons are made with cow fat.

Many **rodeos** feature bulls and calves. In some parts of the world, people burn dried cow **manure** for heat. Farmers also use manure to help plants grow in their fields. In India, some people think cows are **sacred**. There, the animals roam freely.

In Hinduism, cows symbolize life and providence.

Farmers may use ear tags to keep track of individual cows in large herds.

27

DEATH OF A COW

Young cows form friendships and like to stay near their buddies.

With proper care, cows can live as long as 25 years. Most do not live that long. Cows will die, but their young live on. They gallop in pastures. Heifers become cows and have their own calves.

Mother cows quickly develop a strong bond with their calves.

LIFE CYCLE

After 9 months, a cow  gives birth to a calf.

Within an hour of birth, the calf stands up and drinks its mother's milk.

The calf grows quickly and soon eats grass and feed.

 By 8 months, the calf is weaned.

At 1 year old, the heifer weighs about 700 pounds (318 kg).

At 15 months old, the heifer can reproduce.

By the age of 2, the cow gives birth.

The cow gives  birth every 12 to 14 months.

After 7 to 20 years, the cow dies.

GLOSSARY

artificial: *done by humans instead of occurring naturally*

breed: *a group of animals within a species that has similar physical characteristics*

digest: *to turn food into another form*

embryo: *an offspring that has not hatched out of an egg or been born yet*

infections: *sicknesses caused by things like bacteria*

mammals: *warm-blooded animals that usually grow hair or fur and feed their young milk*

manure: *solid waste from animals*

nutrients: *substances needed for growth and to maintain health*

pasture: *a grassy area where farm animals graze*

polled: *describing cattle, sheep, or goats without horns*

regurgitates: *brings swallowed food up to the mouth again*

rodeos: *contests in which cowboys show their skill in events such as riding bulls and roping calves*

sacred: *worthy of religious respect*

wean: *to make a baby used to food other than its mother's milk*

WEBSITES

DK Find Out: Cows
https://www.dkfindout.com/us/animals-and-nature/domesticated-animals/cows/
Read more about cattle and other farm animals.

SciShow Kids: 4 Reasons Cows are Awesome!
https://www.youtube.com/watch?v=m9eqt6YPI7Y
Find out more about different kinds of cows.

Note: Every effort has been made to ensure that the websites listed above are suitable for children, that they have educational value, and that they contain no inappropriate material. However, because of the nature of the Internet, it is impossible to guarantee that these sites will remain active indefinitely or that their contents will not be altered.

READ MORE

Dicker, Katie. *Cow.*
Mankato, Minn.: Smart Apple Media, 2014.

Sexton, Colleen. *The Life Cycle of a Cow.*
Minneapolis: Bellwether Media, 2011.

INDEX

aurochs 25
bodies 7
breeds 7
calves 11, 12, 18, 26, 28, 30
digestion 4, 14, 17
embryos 8
farmers 4, 8, 12, 18, 21, 22, 26
fetuses 8
food 4, 8, 12, 14, 17, 22, 30
herds 21, 22
hooves 4, 7

horns 7
illnesses 21, 22
life span 28, 30
manure 26
mating 18, 30
senses 21
sounds 11
stomachs 4, 17, 22
tails 21
teeth 12, 14